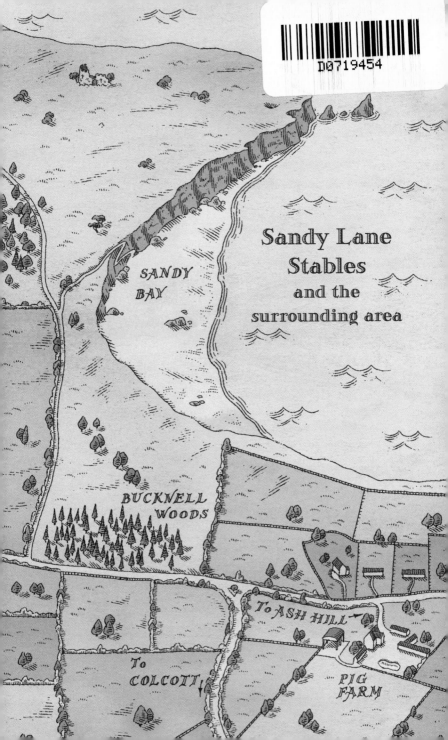

Sandy Lane Stables

Sandy Lane Stables

The Midnight Horse

Michelle Bates

Adapted by: Mary Sebag-Montefiore
Reading consultant: Alison Kelly
Series editor: Lesley Sims
Designed by: Brenda Cole
Cover and inside illustrations: Barbara Bongini
Map illustrations: John Woodcock

This edition first published in 2016 by Usborne Publishing Ltd.,
Usborne House, 83-85 Saffron Hill, London EC1N 8RT, England.
www.usborne.com

Copyright © Usborne Publishing, 2016, 2009, 2003, 1996

Illustrations copyright © Usborne Publishing, 2016

The name Usborne and the devices ♀ ♀ are Trade Marks of
Usborne Publishing Ltd. UKE

A CIP catalogue record for this book is available from the British Library.

Contents

SANDY LANE STABLES

BARN

GATE

STABLE YARD

NICK & SARAH'S COTTAGE

TACK ROOM

OUTDOOR SCHOOL

SANDY LANE

Chapter 1

Izzy

The horse cantered around the paddock in easy, graceful strides, his tail held high, the crest of his neck arched. His jet-black coat gleamed against the white twilight frost; his hooves hardly seemed to touch the cold ground as he danced forwards. On his back a girl, light and balanced, coaxed the reins through her fingers. Effortlessly the pair perfected a figure of eight, before drawing to a halt. The rider swung herself out of the saddle and jumped off.

"That's enough, Midnight," she told him. "It's too dark for us to see now." Gently, she pushed his nose away as he cradled forward for a titbit.

"I've got nothing for you," she smiled. The horse snorted in response, his breath spiralling smoke-like into the wintry air as she led him off.

The horse and his rider looked as if they belonged together. But they didn't. Izzy Paterson didn't own Midnight. And in just over a week's time he was due to be sold...

"A new start for us all," Izzy's father had said when he'd given up his job as a journalist to move to Colcott in the country and write his first book. Izzy had been thrilled. Living in the country could only mean the one thing that mattered to her most – more horses.

Izzy had always been horse-mad. Living in the city meant she'd only had weekly riding lessons. Now things would be much better. Or so she'd thought. But it didn't work out like that. The horse her parents had vaguely talked about buying never materialised. Izzy still only had weekly lessons and now she spent her Saturdays at a riding stables where the riders were a tight-knit group of snooty, unfriendly girls. She didn't feel she fitted in there at all.

"If you improve your marks at school, maybe you can have a horse," her father had said.

But however hard she tried, Izzy couldn't up her marks, any more than she could keep on pretending to her old city friends that her dream horse was on its way. Even her best friend, Alice, had given up asking about him.

Then, like magic, her problems were solved. That wonderful day would stay in her memory forever. The school bus had dropped her as usual by the village shop, and she'd glanced in the window. The advert had jumped out at her:

Would you like to exercise a horse for free?

Rider needed

Phone Mrs. Charlwood

It gave a mobile number. Izzy could hardly believe it. Surely no one... *no one* would let someone ride their horse *for free*. She'd rung immediately, certain there was some sort of mistake. But the offer was totally genuine.

"My daughter, Jane, has got married," Mrs. Charlwood had explained. "Moved to Australia... I couldn't bear to sell Midnight. Try him out if you like. I live at Harewood, the big house on the edge of Colcott."

Izzy had raced there at once. Well-proportioned, part-thoroughbred, with graceful, sloping shoulders, Midnight was in a different league altogether from the riding school ponies she was used to. It wasn't going to be a 'job' looking after him. It was a privilege.

"That's nice, dear," her mother said when Izzy told her the exciting news.

Nice? thought Izzy. *Nice?* For nearly six months Izzy's life was *perfect* – riding weekends, a summer filled with horse shows. Then, one sunny day in June, Mrs. Charlwood dropped the bombshell. She was emigrating to Australia at Christmas.

Izzy was devastated. Her whole world collapsed. Mrs. Charlwood tried to help. She even offered to give Midnight to Izzy, but Izzy's parents had refused.

"Who would end up looking after him?" her mother had said. "Not you. Us. And we can't take on that sort of responsibility just now. Maybe next year we'll get you a horse, Izzy."

But next year seemed a lifetime away. Besides, she didn't want any other horse, only Midnight. Her parents didn't understand. Only Mrs. Charlwood knew how she felt.

"Oh Midnight," she sighed, turning now to face the horse. "How can I live without you?" She took a deep breath. Ordered herself to be brave. It wasn't the end of the world.

But it was. Christmas was only a week away. By then, Mrs. Charlwood would be in Australia with her daughter, Harewood sold, and Midnight gone forever.

"Time to put you away for the night," Izzy sighed, the light around them fading fast. "I mustn't spoil our last days together."

Midnight tossed his head impatiently as Izzy led

him off to the yard. She saw Mrs. Charlwood waving to her from the kitchen window. She smiled back weakly. Leading Midnight into his stable, she began grooming him, brushing his dark coat in swift circular movements.

"All done," she murmured at last, rubbing his velvety nose.

Midnight's head nodded contentedly as Izzy gave him his evening haynet. With one last pat, she closed the stable door behind her and bolted him in for the night. Midnight didn't take his eyes off her. He lifted his head high over the stable door and snickered softly. Izzy swallowed; a lump formed in her throat as she gazed at him. In the luminous twilight, she didn't think she'd ever seen a horse as beautiful.

"You'll be all right Midnight. You'll have a new home. You'll forget me," she whispered, her eyes brimming with tears. "But I'll never forget you."

Chapter 2

Kate

"Come on Kate! It's ten to eight! Up you get. You said you wanted to be at the stables early."

Kate Hardy groaned at the sound of her mother's wake-up call. It was the first day of the Christmas holidays and she was exhausted.

Yawning, she got up and wandered across the room. Pulling a comb through her blonde hair, Kate gazed at herself critically in the mirror. Dark shadows ringed her slate-grey eyes – a consequence of the late nights she'd had finishing her history coursework. Now she wasn't going to waste another thought on it. For the next two weeks, she'd enjoy herself concentrating totally on her riding.

Kate and her brother, Alex, had been helping out at Sandy Lane Stables for nearly three years now: three years of riding, grooming, mucking out and whatever else came along. Though it was hard work, the reward was being with horses. Besides, Nick and Sarah Brooks, the owners of the stables, really appreciated all the extra work their regular riders put in.

This year Kate's efforts had paid off. She had been picked to ride Sandy Lane's star horse, Feather, in the junior section at the Mapletree Horse Trials – now just three weeks away. Made up of dressage, showjumping and cross-country, the trials were the winter event of the area and the opportunity Kate had been waiting for. Everyone else at the stables had excelled at some point in the past... now it was her turn. This was her chance to prove herself. She was determined – she *had* to win.

Last night, Nick had said, "I think you're in with

a real chance."

Kate smiled, remembering. She wasn't a conceited girl. She knew that the other regular Sandy Lane riders would have been competing if they'd been young enough to enter. Tom, Jess, Charlie, Rosie, even her brother Alex were all better riders, but they were too old. So Sandy Lane's hopes were riding on her.

Kate drew her bedroom curtains. Snow lay thick on the ground and little icicles hung precariously from the window ledge. Kate was pleased. That meant she'd be in the all-weather outdoor school, working on dressage, her favourite discipline.

Quickly she glanced at her bedside clock. Five to eight. She'd been daydreaming again. She'd better hurry or she'd be late. She'd promised to be at the stables for eight to help Nick feed the horses. Struggling into her jodhpurs, she grabbed her riding hat and raced down the stairs. Alex was already in the kitchen, crunching toast.

"Mum, ple-e-ase, give us a lift to Sandy Lane?"

Kate called, grabbing some bread. "Just this once?"

"What's wrong with the bus?"

"That'll take ages. I don't want to be late. Please?" Kate begged.

Mrs. Hardy considered. "OK, Kate. But it will be just this once. You'll have to get up earlier if you want to be on time. You can't rely on me."

"Thanks Mum," Kate said, gratefully.

"Have you got all your Christmas presents sorted out?" Mrs. Hardy asked.

Kate nodded, smiling as she thought of the riding crop she'd bought Alex. Tanned leather with a shiny handle. Perfect. It had cost her a big chunk of her savings. When she remembered how they squabbled, she wasn't sure he deserved it.

They slid across the snow to the car, and in no time at all, Mrs. Hardy had dropped Kate and Alex in Sandy Lane. Kate looked at her phone. Twenty five past eight. They were late. Passing the line of conifers that enclosed the outdoor school, they walked on into the yard.

Kate could see Charlie filling water buckets by the trough in the corner of the yard, and Rosie and Jess were deep in conversation by the barn. She hoped her late arrival hadn't been noticed as she hurried to collect some grooming kit. But it hadn't escaped Charlie, and he called over to Kate as she dived into the tack room.

"Overslept, did you?" he called. "Nick's been looking everywhere for you."

Kate pretended she hadn't heard him. She liked Charlie but she wasn't in the mood for any comments like that from him this morning. Hurrying over to Feather's stable, she drew back the bolt. The Arab mare snickered softly as Kate set to work on grooming her coat.

When she'd finished, Kate stood back to admire her handiwork. She was a perfectionist, but even she couldn't fault Feather's appearance. Just at that moment Nick Brooks looked in.

"What happened to you this morning, Kate?"

"Sorry Nick, I overslept," Kate answered.

"No worries," Nick said. "Not with the way you've made Feather look. You've worked hard to get her gleaming like that. We won't risk going out over the cross-country course in this weather," he went on. "So I'll look at your dressage test in the outdoor school instead."

"Brilliant," Kate replied. Just as she'd hoped.

"Meet you down there in five minutes."

"Yes, Nick." Kate tacked Feather up and led the horse out of her stable. Springing neatly into the saddle, she headed off to the all-weather outdoor school. Feather's ears were pricked, alert and attentive, as she sniffed the air.

"All ready?" asked Nick, stamping his feet to ward off the cold as he opened the gate to let her into the school. "Can you remember it all?" he called.

"I think so," Kate said, casting her mind back over her dressage test. She didn't want to sound boastful, but in truth, she knew it like the back of her hand. She even dreamt about it.

"Good. Now, trot Feather around the school to

warm up and then we'll begin," Nick said. "We've got a lot of work to put in before Mapletree."

Kate nudged Feather on into a trot.

"Shall I start now?" she called. Nick nodded.

Tentatively, she gave the obligatory salute to the imaginary judges, feeling embarrassed that no one was there. Then she urged Feather on to make her way down the long side of the white railings at a trot. Feather didn't even falter as Kate prompted her forward and they swept across the diagonal, slicing through the centre of the ring.

Kate sat deep into the saddle, feeling at ease as she brought Feather to a walk. One, two, three. Kate counted the numbers in her head before pushing Feather on into a canter. So far so good. Now just once around the railings on a free rein.

"Circle, change the rein, same on the other leg," she muttered to herself as she squeezed Feather on into a trot. Taking care not to hurry the last section, she came down the centre line and halted in the middle of the school before reining back. One, two, three steps... stop. They had made it through the test easily. Riding Feather was like dancing with the perfect partner and no matter what Nick thought, Kate had enjoyed herself. She looked up expectantly.

Nick clapped loudly. "Excellent," he said. "You forgot just one thing."

"Did I?" What could she have forgotten?

"The salute for the judges at the end."

Kate sighed. "It's weird to remember to do it when they're not there."

"Get into the habit now. Then you won't have to think about it on the day," Nick said, adding, "Don't look so worried. You did well. If we can get your showjumping and cross-country up to that standard, you'll have a chance. OK if I leave you to work on your walk to canter transitions, while I sign everyone in for the ten o'clock hack?"

"Sure. And... thank you."

"That's fine," said Nick. "I want you to win. No pressure." He winked. "But if you do win, Feather becomes even more valuable for Sandy Lane Stables.

Although I'd never sell her," he promised, seeing Kate's anxious face. "See you later."

Kate practised as Nick suggested and gradually Feather's movements became more fluid. As she finally reined back, she felt pleased. She'd done her best. They were working well together. And tomorrow she'd concentrate on showjumping. She began to hum contentedly to herself.

Chapter 3

A Hasty Decision

Izzy stared vacantly out of the bedroom window. First day of the Christmas holidays. It shouldn't be miserable, but it was. The snow was so deep, she couldn't even ride. Midnight would be sold by Friday. There had to be a way around it. There had to be something she could do to stop him from going to the sale. If only she could find the money to pay the livery fee herself. But how?

She'd been hours, she thought, doing nothing but staring and staring out of the window.

The more Izzy thought about her life without

Midnight, the worse it seemed. In the summer, Christmas had seemed so far away. Something, she'd been certain, would save him. Now time had almost run out for them both. Panic rose in her throat. What would she do without him?

Maybe she should try talking to her father again one last time.

He was supposed to be going up to London today. She'd make him some lunch before he went. That would put him in a good mood.

Cheese on toast was easy enough. Tiptoeing around the kitchen so as not to disturb him, she prepared it carefully and put it under the grill. Then she wandered into the sitting room and picked up a horsy magazine.

Bleeep... bleeep... bleeep... bleeep... bleeep!

A shrill, piercing sound filled the house. The smoke alarm!

"NO-OO." Izzy whizzed into the kitchen. Her father would not be happy.

She tugged the tray of burnt offerings out of the

grill as her father shot in from his study amid clouds of smoke.

"What are you doing?" he bellowed over the high pitched whistles. Izzy held her hands over her ears while he tried to stop the noise. At last, he yanked the battery out of the alarm. He looked furious.

"I've got to leave in five minutes and I smell of burnt toast."

"Sorry Dad. I was only– I just want to say–"

Hopeless. Mr. Paterson was already halfway up the stairs, taking two at a time.

Izzy had to talk to him before he left.

"Dad. Listen," she started, as he reappeared, freshly changed, at the top of the stairs.

"Not now, Izzy," he said, heading downstairs and striding to the front door.

"It's about Midnight. I've got to speak to you before it's too late."

"Too late!" Izzy froze under his look of fury. "We've already decided. The answer's no. That's final." He slammed the door behind him.

The sound echoed in Izzy's head. She heard the car zoom off. She was alone. Her mother wouldn't be back for ages. She had a new job, which meant working on Saturdays. Miserably, Izzy started leafing through the local newspaper. And then she saw the advert. "Mapletree Horse Trials, Saturday 11th January. Dressage, cross-country and showjumping," she read. "New junior event for under 12s. First prize £200."

Izzy clutched the newspaper, crumpling the pages. *Mapletree Horse Trials... £200.*

She went upstairs to her bedroom. As the door closed behind her, she let out a sigh. Her mind raced. That prize money would tide her over, wouldn't it? Pay for at least a month's livery fee? But January 11th was three weeks away and by then Midnight would be sold.

Then she had an idea. Quick as a flash, she raced downstairs and crept into her father's study. Before she had a chance to change her mind, she turned on his computer, punched in his password and started to type.

Dear Mrs. Charlwood, she wrote carefully. She took a deep breath, before launching in.

It was very kind of you to offer my daughter, Izzy, your horse, Midnight. She paused to read what she had written. It sounded good.

As you know, she adores him, so it was very hard for me to say no. Unfortunately, my wife and I have been so busy that we didn't think we'd have the time to help her look after him. Now, however, I can see light at the end of the tunnel, and I should have my book finished by Christmas. Izzy's schoolwork is improving and...

Here Izzy felt the first twinge of guilt. Only a small lie, she comforted herself – her English marks were a bit better. She continued *...as it's almost Christmas I thought it would be nice if Izzy could have Midnight – if you are still willing. She told me that he hasn't been sold yet, but is due to go to the Ash Hill sale on Friday. I tried to phone yesterday to talk things through, but couldn't get hold of you. Izzy was so anxious for it to be sorted out as soon as possible that I said I* *would write and let her bring the letter to you in person.*

Thank you so much for all the kindness you have shown Izzy over the past year and the very best of luck with your big move.

Yours sincerely, she finished triumphantly. Perfect. Quickly she pressed 'print', grabbed a pen, signing her father's name with a flourish: *Maximilian Paterson.* Then she deleted the document. No one would ever know.

Izzy looked at her phone. Half two. The sooner she knew the answer the better. She flung on her jacket, grabbed a scarf and set off.

Soon she was at Mrs. Charlwood's door. She rang the bell. Waited. For a moment she wondered if Mrs. Charlwood was out and her plan would fail. She felt a glimmer of relief. Then the door opened.

"Izzy! How lovely!" Mrs. Charlwood said. "I didn't expect to see you today."

"I've just had the most amazing news! I can hardly believe it!" Izzy gabbled. "It's this letter!"

"Slow down, Izzy." Mrs. Charlwood looked

puzzled. "What letter?"

"From my father," Izzy said breathlessly, handing it over. "He says I can have Midnight."

"Really? That's wonderful." Mrs. Charlwood read the letter eagerly. "I wonder why your father changed his mind."

Izzy squirmed uncomfortably.

"Doesn't matter," Mrs. Charlwood went on. "If he says you can have Midnight, of course you must. I'll just phone him to confirm."

Izzy's heart thumped and she felt the blood rising to her head. "Oh, but you can't, Mrs. Charlwood!"

The words tumbled out before she had a chance to stop herself.

Mrs. Charlwood looked surprised. And then Izzy relaxed as she remembered there wasn't anyone at home. "I mean... I mean... Dad's just on his way up to London for a business meeting and he won't want to be disturbed on his mobile."

Mrs. Charlwood thought long and hard. "Well, I suppose I can ring him later. You and I can decide where to keep him, can't we?"

"Yes." Izzy smiled and exhaled slowly with relief. She'd got away with it for now, and she could fend off any further threats. Mrs. Charlwood was so busy with her move, she might easily forget to ring.

"Where does your father want you to keep him?" Mrs. Charlwood asked.

Izzy hesitated. "H-He said I should sort something out with you."

"What about Sandy Lane Stables? Have you heard of it?"

Izzy shook her head.

"It's got an excellent reputation," said Mrs. Charlwood. "I know the owner, Nick Brooks. He's a superb rider... a top steeplechase jockey. He taught my Jane to ride. Jane lost her nerve after a bad fall and Nick managed to restore her confidence in horses. He married a few years ago and set up Sandy Lane. His wife, Sarah, is as nice as Nick," Mrs. Charlwood rambled on.

"It sounds brilliant," Izzy said. Suddenly the sheer

craziness of her scheme hit her. She couldn't pay Midnight's livery right now. The Mapletree Horse Trials weren't until the 11th January. And she might not win. But now Mrs. Charlwood was going on about how wonderful Sandy Lane was and how happy Midnight would be there.

Izzy had to think fast.

"There's just one small problem," she mumbled. "Dad said he can't pay for a livery fee until the end of January when he gets paid for his book."

"Oh dear," Mrs. Charlwood looked thoughtful. "That is a difficulty… I'll give Nick a ring now and see if we can work something out. Why don't you go and see Midnight? I'll meet you by his stable."

"Thanks," Izzy said gratefully, blushing furiously. She crunched through the snow to the stable yard. She felt sick. How could she have lied like that? And to Mrs. Charlwood of all people? She still had time to race to the house and tell the truth.

Midnight was looking out over his box. He whinnied loudly at her approach. No, it was too late.

She didn't have it in her to turn back – not now. She couldn't give him up. Fishing around in her pocket, she pulled out a sugar lump.

"Here you are Midnight," she crooned as he nuzzled into her hand.

"All settled," a voice called from behind her. Izzy turned around quickly.

"Nick says you can pay at the end of the month, as long as you don't forget!" joked Mrs. Charlwood. "Not that that's likely. Nick's thrilled to be getting you both. I'll arrange for Midnight to be boxed and sent over as soon as possible. No, don't worry about the cost." She held up her hand to silence Izzy. "I'm glad to do it. I never wanted him to be sold. I'd rather he went to you than anyone else. He couldn't have a better owner." Mrs. Charlwood hurried off. She had a mountain of packing to do.

Izzy stood outside Midnight's stable. She felt awful. Midnight was hers, yet as soft flakes of snow began to settle on her jacket, she felt as if the weight of the world was bearing down on her.

Chapter 4

A New Arrival

"Good news, everyone," Nick called across the yard. "We've got a new horse arriving at Sandy Lane this afternoon."

"Whose is he?" Tom asked.

"Well," Nick hesitated. "He belongs to an old friend of mine – a Mrs. Charlwood, and she's given the horse away to–"

"GIVEN him away?" squealed Kate.

"Don't look so shocked," Nick laughed. "He was her daughter Jane's horse but Jane's grown up. She moved to Australia and Mrs. Charlwood's emigrating to join her. So she's given him to the girl who's been looking after him for the last year – Izzy Paterson. Any of you know her?"

The riders all looked blankly at each other and shook their heads.

"She lives in Colcott; she's about your age, Kate."

"Well, she's not in my class at school," Kate said. "I wonder what she's like."

"Anyone Mrs. Charlwood thinks fit to give Midnight to must be pretty special," Nick went on. "He's an amazing showjumper. Jane won loads of prizes with him. It'll be good to have some new talent at the stables and as he's only being kept on at half-livery, we'll be able to use him in lessons."

"And is this Izzy an amazing rider too?" Tom asked, sounding concerned.

"Worried about the competition, Tom?" Charlie teased him.

"I was just asking," Tom spluttered, embarrassed.

"My information stops here," said Nick. "You'll have to wait and see. Come on everyone, let's get going. We have to get the spare box ready for him and the midday hack's going out in a moment."

Kate turned back to Feather's stable. It didn't take her long to tack up the little grey Arab and soon she was leading her out of the stable.

"Ready to ride to the lighthouse?" Sarah, Nick's wife, called from where she was standing with Storm Cloud.

"Yes," chorused the riders.

"Then off we go!" Sarah headed into the icy wind, followed by the hacking group. As they trotted, Kate was noticing how her friends paired up. Jess and Rosie were inseparable. Alex and Tom had been best mates for years. Charlie had always fitted in anywhere. But what about her? Kate was acutely aware that she was the youngest. Though everyone made an effort to include her, she was often on her own. Maybe this new girl would be a real friend.

"Wake up, Kate," Sarah smiled.

Kate nudged Feather on into a trot and soon they were at Sandy Lane Cove.

"We're going to have a canter," Sarah called, drawing to a halt at the top of the cliffs to wait for the last of them. "Take it easy."

One by one the riders streamed forward. Kate followed on behind the others at the back. The little grey horse's hooves drummed as they flew over the hard ground. Kate's face stung with cold. She lowered her head to shield herself from the wind, feeling adrenaline surge through her.

Nothing could be as amazing as riding. She knew that as surely as she breathed. Winding back along the coastal track, Kate felt she was floating in happiness. Clattering into the yard with the others, she saw Nick waiting patiently. When everyone was gathered together, he led out a black horse.

The horse arched his neck, blowing softly through his nostrils. As he walked forward, he nuzzled Nick's hand. He was magnificent. Jet-black from head to toe with just the tiniest sprinklings of white hairs forming a star on his forehead.

"What's his name?" Kate asked.

"It's a long story," Nick laughed, patting the horse's shoulder fondly. "I've always called him The Midnight Horse. I was lodging with the Charlwoods when I first met him. He was kept out in the fields behind the house. He used to gallop around at night trying to get out, and whenever I asked who he belonged to, or why no one ever came to ride him, everyone kept quiet. That's when I first started calling him The Midnight Horse. Later, I found out that Jane Charlwood had lost her nerve in an accident and wouldn't ride any more. So I decided I'd help Jane ride again... and I did."

Nick smiled at the memories. "The Midnight Horse stuck, and then it was shortened to Midnight. He's just as I remembered him. Mrs. Charlwood never wanted to sell him. I suppose, by giving him to Izzy Paterson, she hasn't."

Lucky Izzy Paterson, Kate thought to herself as she admired the black horse. Yes, the name Midnight suited him perfectly.

"Did Izzy come with him?" she asked.

"No, he was just delivered. She'll be here later, I'm sure."

"I wish I could ride him, just once," Kate murmured, but Nick overheard.

"How about the ten o'clock hack on Friday? Provided his owner hasn't got plans to ride him then herself of course."

"Brilliant," said Kate quickly, racing to Feather's stable so Nick couldn't change his mind.

As she groomed Feather, she gazed at Midnight, his head silhouetted against the sky. He was truly beautiful. Why hadn't his owner come? She couldn't love him very much if she was happy to leave him to settle alone in a new place.

Midnight whinnied loudly. Kate slipped into his stable to give him a reassuring pat.

"I won't let you be lonely," she promised him. "I'll look after you."

She had Christmas to look forward to. And after that, a ride on Midnight.

Chapter 5

The Midnight Horse

Christmas was a whirl of excitement. Kate got a beautiful pair of riding gloves from Alex, which made her thankful that she'd been generous with his riding crop. What with games, crackers, jokes and laughter, Kate wished the day would never end.

"How was Christmas?" Nick called as she came into the yard the day after Christmas.

"Good," she answered. "Except I ate too much! How's Midnight?"

"Fine."

"And his owner?"

"Not turned up yet."

Kate sighed with relief. With luck, she could ride him in the ten o'clock hack.

"I don't have her phone number to see where she's got to and I can't ask Mrs. Charlwood, because she's already left the country," worried Nick. "I'll check the phone book."

Kate trailed Nick into the tack room where he flicked through the pages. "No Patersons listed. They must be ex-directory."

"So I can ride him?" Kate asked anxiously.

"OK," Nick grinned. "Tack up."

Kate raced across the yard, drew back the bolt to Midnight's stable and ran her hand down his sleek, polished neck.

"Lovely boy," she whispered. She leant against his shoulder, lifting each of his hooves to pick them out. His head nodded contentedly as she groomed him quickly and led him out, noticing, with satisfaction, everyone's admiring glances.

"Where's he come from?"

"He's new," Kate answered. "He's called Midnight. Isn't he beautiful?"

She put her foot into the stirrup iron, sprang lightly into the saddle, and gathered up the reins.

"Who does he belong to?"

"A girl called Izzy Paterson, but she hasn't turned up yet," Kate answered.

"All ready?" Nick called, walking forward on Whispering Silver. He looked around him at the group of riders.

As they clattered out of the yard, Kate settled down to his long, easy stride.

"Trot on," Nick called.

One by one the riders kicked their mounts forward. Kate squeezed her calves very lightly and Midnight went into a trot. He was wonderful to ride. Kate looked around her. The snow had disappeared and though she was sad to see it go, Kate was glad they could go out hacking again. As the riders slowed their pace back down to a walk, the ponies' breaths came short and sharp in the crisp winter air. The sharp scent of pine trees engulfed Kate and she took a gulp of air. She sat tight to the saddle as they cantered through the trees and popped over a fallen log. She couldn't think of any place she'd rather be than out riding on Midnight.

"Atishooo!" Izzy Paterson sat up as her mother opened the door to her bedroom, carrying a mug.

"Drink this, Izzy."

Izzy groaned. Her head slumped back onto the pillow, as she shivered and sweated simultaneously. "I feel better now," she lied. "Maybe I can get up."

Mrs. Paterson frowned. "I don't think so," she said. "The doctor said you have 'flu pretty badly. Said you need to stay in bed for a week, remember?"

Izzy closed her eyes. She felt helpless.

"What's the matter?" Mrs. Paterson asked. "Are you still upset about that horse?"

"N-no," Izzy said, flooded by a wave of guilt.

"Is it because you're missing tonight's party at your cousins'? They can visit you next week."

"Mum, that's the last thing I want," Izzy moaned, rolling onto her side. "I've got nothing in common with Holly and Melanie. I hate talking about clothes and they think I'm crazy when I talk about horses."

She couldn't tell her mother the real reason for her despair – that this was the fourth day away from a horse she wasn't even supposed to have. Izzy stared miserably out of the window.

Her mother sighed. "You will be all right here on your own, won't you?"

Izzy nodded.

"Mrs. Watson from next door said she'll call in on you in half an hour, and we won't be long."

"OK," Izzy said. Mrs. Paterson closed the door behind her.

Izzy sighed. She was determined to see Midnight, but she'd have to wait until Mrs. Watson came and went before she could even think about doing anything. Izzy lay very still, trying to gather energy into herself.

At last, Mrs. Watson arrived and made her another

hot drink, fussing around her like a mother hen.

"I'll leave you now, dear," Mrs. Watson said kindly. "You must be tired."

Izzy nodded, feeling guilty that she hadn't made any effort at conversation. She waited till she heard the door slam. Then she struggled out of bed and into her clothes.

Feeling giddy she fumbled her way down the stairs, grabbed her jacket and shut the door behind her before finding her bike. She knew she wasn't really well enough, but she had to see Midnight. Swaying dizzily as she turned the pedals on her bike, she gripped the handle bars and set off down the road. It was amazing what you could make yourself do, she found, when you were totally determined.

Eight o'clock. The cold night air sent a chill running through her body and Izzy shivered. It wasn't a long way, but it seemed to take forever. At last she saw the sign for the stables and swung in.

All was quiet. Luckily, no one was about. Noiselessly, she glanced into a stable... Not there.

And then she heard a loud whinny, a whinny she instantly recognized. *Midnight!* Spinning around, she saw the black horse's familiar face looking out over a stable door.

"Ssh my boy," she said, rushing over. "You'll wake up the whole yard." She drew back the bolt and stepped inside.

"I can't stay with you long, Midnight," she said, burying her head in his mane. "I'm not even supposed to be out, but I just had to see you. Don't worry, I'll be back soon. After all, we've got a lot of work to do if we're going to be fit for Mapletree," she wheezed. "I'm ill, and I'm sorry because I'll have to leave you now, but I'll be back again tomorrow to look after you properly."

The horse whinnied softly as Izzy turned to go. Shivering in the cold air, she set off back home. She hadn't had long with Midnight, and she felt even worse than when she had left the house, but at least she had seen him – that made all the difference. And surely she'd feel better tomorrow.

Chapter 6

Another Competitor

Izzy didn't feel any better the next day, or the next. Her night time escapade had set her back, and she wasn't allowed out until Monday. Although she was desperate to see Midnight, she felt nervous at the prospect of turning up at the stables.

"Just go along, Izzy," Mrs. Charlwood had said, "You'll be fine. Nick will look after you."

Mrs. Charlwood had made it sound easy, but she was on the other side of the world now. Izzy was alone, with a web of deception.

"Stay calm, look confident," she told herself. But

as she entered the yard, calm and confident was the last thing Izzy felt.

The yard looked busy; people were running around chattering excitedly, laughing and joking. Izzy wanted to creep away. She took a deep breath and forced herself to walk forward.

Kate didn't see Izzy. She was too busy with Midnight. This was the fourth day she had been looking after him and he was beginning to recognize her. As she groomed him, she let her mind replay the last few days. Nick had been right. He really was a dream to ride.

"OK boy?" Kate said, patting his black neck. "I'll get you tacked up."

As she crossed the yard to collect his saddle, Kate saw a girl walking towards her.

"Hi. Can I help you?" she asked, politely.

"Possibly," the girl answered. "I'm looking for Nick Brooks. Do you know where he is?"

"He's in his cottage, the other side of the yard," Kate answered.

"Thanks. I'm Izzy Paterson," the girl announced.

Kate stared. "We've been expecting you since before Christmas."

"I've been ill. I've had flu," Izzy spoke sharply. "Where's my horse?"

She didn't even smile. Kate took an instant dislike to her.

A stilted silence hung in the air. For a brief moment, the two girls frowned at each other, and then Kate remembered her manners.

"I'll take you to him," she said, "He's over here,"

Kate drew back the bolt to his stable and stood back as Izzy pushed in. The horse gave a whinny of recognition.

"Silly old boy," Izzy crooned.

Kate looked on enviously, feeling strangely distant. Midnight obviously knew who he belonged to. She went to find Nick.

Nick hurried over to the box. "I'm Nick Brooks," he introduced himself. "You're Izzy Paterson?" Kate hung back, watching.

"Yes. I'm sorry I didn't come before, but I was ill."

"No worries. Kate's taken good care of Midnight," Nick said. "Now, if you'll give me your phone number, I can put it up on the tack room notice board with the others."

"I can't," Izzy snapped. As Nick raised his eyebrows, she wished she'd produced a smoother reply. "I, um, I don't have a mobile at the moment," she mumbled, crossing her fingers, "and my Dad's a writer. He hates being disturbed. He won't let anyone ring home. I'm sorry, but I can't help it."

Nick frowned. "I'm afraid I must have all our owners' numbers," he insisted, holding out a pad of paper. "For emergencies."

Reluctantly Izzy said, "OK." To Kate, it sounded like sulkiness.

"There's a hack going out at ten o'clock. Would you like to join it?" Nick asked.

"Sure," Izzy said, turning back to Midnight.

This girl was *rude*. How could anyone talk so dismissively to Nick? There was something odd about Izzy Paterson, Kate decided. Bitterly disappointed – she'd been hoping to ride Midnight herself – she went to find Alex. He was in Napoleon's stable, just where she'd expected.

"Midnight's owner has arrived," Kate told him. "Izzy Paterson. She's finally made it."

"What's she like?" he asked.

"A bit of a spoilt brat, I think," said Kate. "You should have heard the way she spoke to Nick. She made some excuse about 'flu."

Alex laughed. "Well, maybe she really was ill. Give her the benefit of the doubt. Let's get ready for the hack."

"I was going to ride Midnight and now I can't," Kate pouted. She could hear the petulance in her voice, but was powerless to stop it. "Who does she think she is, breezing in here?"

"Midnight's owner?" Alex said, with a grin. "Come on. Let's go."

"OK," Kate snapped. Quickly she got Feather ready and led her out of her box.

Kate was watching Izzy's every move as they rode off. She looked a natural. Midnight was perfectly on the bit and Izzy's seat looked just right.

"How long have you been riding, Izzy?" Kate asked, taking Feather up alongside her.

"Only properly this last year – since I've had Midnight. But I've had lessons on and off for the last five years, although that's not the same as having your own horse, is it?" Izzy knew she was babbling.

"Probably not," Kate said, enviously. She'd often wondered what it would be like to own a horse.

"Canter over the log," Nick called from the front, disturbing Kate's thoughts.

One by one, the riders turned their horses and took them over the fallen tree trunk. Kate spurred Feather on and the little grey mare responded, soaring over the jump.

Kate started to relax. Cantering across the grassy scrub, the wind whipped up snatches of conversation and sent stray words down the line of horses.

"Kate's the only one entered... two weeks away."

Kate's heart started to beat faster. Was Nick talking about Mapletree? Nudging Feather forwards, she trotted on until she was within earshot of Izzy and Nick.

"I've been training Kate for a couple of months now, but another representative from Sandy Lane wouldn't go amiss."

Another Sandy Lane representative? What did Nick mean? Kate's heart skipped a beat.

"Hi, Kate," Nick said, turning in the saddle towards her. "I've been telling Izzy you're entered for Mapletree. Izzy's entered as well, so you can train together."

Kate's smile froze on her face. This was going to be *her* chance to prove herself. Now here was Izzy, hardly five minutes at Sandy Lane, and already pushing her way in. Kate didn't want to share Mapletree with anyone, let alone this unpleasant girl. She felt drenched in a cloud of gloom. She longed to ride fast, to speed off, to forget what she had heard. She fought back tears. Pulling at Feather's head, she circled the little grey horse who was struggling against her reins. And then Kate released her and urged her forward.

"Let's go," she cried. Tears streamed from her eyes and they raced faster and faster. As they battled with the wind, all Kate could hear was the pounding of Feather's hooves. Now she felt better. Riding always did that for her; it filled her with joy and power and determination. She was going to be... not just good at riding, but the best. She was going to win at Mapletree.

Chapter 7

Settling In

Izzy's feelings of dread coming to Sandy Lane seemed far away now. Her plan was succeeding. She'd told her parents she was helping out at a local riding stables – and they'd believed her without question. Everything was working out.

All the Sandy Lane people were incredibly friendly, except Kate. Ever since Nick had mentioned Mapletree, Kate had been distinctly unfriendly.

"I won't be upset," Izzy told herself, although deep down, she was. "I'll just concentrate on riding. Mapletree is only a week away."

Izzy slipped into Midnight's stable and began to tack him up.

"Breathe in," she whispered. "You're putting on weight. It must be all those extra oats I've been feeding you."

She led him out into the yard to join the others. Kate was busy tightening Feather's girth and Tom was already on Chancey. Alex was leading Hector out and Charlie was ambling around the yard on Napoleon. It was New Year's Eve and everyone was excited. Tom was having them all over to his house that evening. Izzy had been invited too. She felt they must like her now – everyone, that is, except Kate.

They headed off to the outdoor school.

"Let's get warmed up. I've laid out a course for you to try," announced Nick.

Izzy looked at the painted fences. It was a simple figure of eight course. The hardest fence was probably the triple, coming so close after the parallel bars, but she didn't think Midnight would have a problem with that. She was so busy working out her route that she only caught Nick's last instructions.

"So I propose that Alex tries Napoleon, Charlie rides Feather and Jess and Rosie do a simple swap. Tom can ride Midnight and Izzy can try Chancey. And Kate, you can ride Hector."

"What did he say, Tom?" whispered Izzy.

"We're switching around," Tom whispered back, "so we don't get used to riding one horse. Nick thinks we get lazy. He's right of course. I know all Chancey's tricks."

Izzy gulped, sick with nerves. She hadn't ridden another horse in ages.

"Tom, take the lead," Nick called, once they had limbered up their mounts.

Steadily, Tom turned Midnight to the start and they skimmed over the first two jumps with ease. Tom turned him wide for the staircase, urging him up and over and onto the gate. They cleared that and then the parallel bars, landing lightly before the triple bar. Now there was only the double.

"One, two, three, jump," Izzy muttered to herself

as she watched keenly. He was over the second part of the double. That was a clear round. Izzy felt a stab of pride at the ripple of applause for her Midnight.

"He's wonderful to ride, Izzy," smiled Tom.

"That was very good, Tom," Nick said. "Your turn now, Kate."

Kate picked up her reins and urged Hector on to the first, taking him around the course at a lumbering pace. Still, she jumped clear.

Izzy felt her nerves tightening as, one by one, after their names were called, each rider performed. The better they rode, the more anxious she felt. Her palms were clammy as she gripped the reins. To her horror, Chancey sensed her uncertainty; he was hotting up as he pawed at the ground.

"Give him a pat; that'll calm him," Tom advised her. "He just hates waiting. Here's a tip – try not to check his stride before you take off. He doesn't need much lead."

"OK," Izzy tried to sound calm. But Tom's words made her feel worse. She didn't know how she'd manage to get round. As she watched Jess draw to a halt, with one fence down, she realized that Nick was calling her name.

"Izzy, Izzy, can you hear me?"

"Sorry." Izzy blushed. She circled Chancey at a canter and began the course. She was so concerned with trying to get Chancey to look at the jump that she completely forgot Tom's advice. Chancey flung his head high into the air and they took off too early. Izzy had completely misjudged it and found herself hanging in mid-air. She hit the saddle with an ungainly thud.

Gritting her teeth, she rode on and placed Chancey at the sharks' teeth. They jumped that clear and turned to the staircase, but Chancey was fighting her every step of the way. Izzy wasn't enjoying it, which the chestnut horse fully understood, and he tore forward, cutting corners and heading out of control. Izzy felt her arms nearly torn out of their sockets as they clipped the staircase and rode at the gate. Her confidence evaporated at every turn. She knew she hadn't given Chancey enough time to look at the jump and he skidded to a halt, his heels digging firmly into the ground. First refusal. Izzy turned him for a second attempt. She hurried him, anxious to get it over. Same again. Second refusal.

"I don't think he's going over that today, Izzy," Nick called kindly. "Try him at the parallel."

Trying to collect herself, Izzy rode him over the parallel and went on to jump the triple bar before heading for the double. One, two and they were over. But by the time they had finished, she felt completely shattered.

"Don't worry," Tom said as she returned to the group. "He takes a bit of getting used to. He did that to me when I first rode him. He gets very fresh if he's kept waiting."

Izzy nodded. Chancey had calmed down now and stood still. She jumped off and returned him to Tom. As she collected Midnight and led him back to his stable, a wave of panic shot through her. She hadn't done well. She'd let herself down. What if she rode that badly at Mapletree?

If she didn't win at Mapletree, she wouldn't be able to pay what she owed.

"Oh, Midnight," she cried, alone in his stable. "What am I going to do?" She couldn't bring herself to leave him.

Kate's face, appearing over the stable door, startled her.

"Did you want something?" Izzy snapped, furious with herself for almost letting Kate hear her. Did Kate suspect anything?

Her problems seemed to be mounting up.

"I wanted to check Midnight was OK," Kate answered. "You've been in there for ages."

"He's fine," Izzy answered, tersely. "Everything's just fine."

"Right. Well, I'm off. See you later at Tom's," Kate said, striding away.

Izzy couldn't tell if Kate believed her or not.

Chapter 8

Rivals

New Year's Day turned out to be dark and gloomy. Not a good start to the year, Kate thought to herself as she sat alone in the tack room. The sky looked tumultuous and forbidding, black clouds scudding back and forth. Still, yesterday evening had been fun. She rubbed her eyes, finding it hard to keep awake after the late night festivities.

Kate put some saddle soap on her sponge and cast her mind back over the last few days. She and Izzy were going to train with Nick over the cross-country course that afternoon, and Kate didn't feel much like going out with her at all. Izzy was so prickly. She seemed to shove away any friendliness Kate tried to show. It was really difficult to get along.

The sound of footsteps in the yard interrupted her thoughts. She looked out of the tack room window. Izzy. The last person she wished to see. The others were all out on a hack – she'd have to be alone with her.

The tack room door swung open.

"I didn't know you were here, Kate," Izzy said. Her voice was cold and hard, Kate thought. "Where is everyone?"

"Sarah's up at the house." Kate tried to sound noncommittal. "The others are out on the two o'clock hack. Nick said to give Feather's saddle a clean before the cross-country this afternoon."

"Then I ought to do Midnight's," Izzy said. "I'll join you."

An uncomfortable silence filled the room as the two girls sat, furiously polishing away at their tack.

"What time did Nick say he'd take us out?"

Izzy said at last.

"Three," Kate answered, not looking up.

"It's ten to," Izzy said, looking at her watch. "I'll get Midnight ready now. See you at the course."

"OK," said Kate, making her way purposefully to Feather's stable with a gleaming saddle, and tacking up the grey mare. She led her into the yard and trotted round to warm her up, before heading off to the cross-country course.

She knew the course wasn't difficult. It didn't provide the variety of jumps that Mapletree would have, but it would be good practice all the same.

Eventually she heard voices: Izzy on Midnight and Nick on Whispering Silver, ambling through the gate. She rode over to them, watching them. They were chatting easily together. She could feel irritation spreading over her like an itchy rash.

"Let's get started," Nick said as she approached. "Remember to ride carefully out there. It's still slippery and I don't want you breaking your necks."

"OK," Kate said, her eyes glued to the course.

"Would you like to go first, Kate, while Izzy gets Midnight warmed up?" Nick suggested.

Kate nodded and nudged Feather on for the brush. Lightly they thundered across the dirt, over the hayrack, before galloping on. They flew over the hedge and into the woods as if they were point-to-pointing. They were going fast... too fast. But something made Kate kick Feather on even more and they raced to the log pile in the trees. Still, Kate didn't slow Feather's pace.

The grey horse hurtled forward at breakneck speed, straining at the bit. Clear of the tyres, they turned to take the zigzag rails in their stride. Up the hill and over the low gate, they raced, pounding forwards for the stone wall.

Feather's sides were heaving in and out like bellows as she cleared the last jump with inches to spare and sprinted back to Nick and Izzy.

As Kate drew to a halt she felt uneasy. They had gone dangerously fast. Deep down, Kate knew it perfectly well.

"Hmm." Nick looked down at his stopwatch, his expression less than pleased. "That was very quick, Kate. You must have cut a few corners in the woods to notch up that speed."

Kate felt herself grow red. Nick was right.

"Your turn, Izzy," Nick instructed.

Izzy nodded, giving Kate a hard stare as she turned towards the first jump. The black horse thundered across the ground. Kate watched, keen-eyed. Izzy sat tight to the saddle and they flew over the tiger trap and onto the brush. Then they raced over the hayrack and onto the hedge into the trees. Kate held her breath, waiting to catch sight of them again. One, two, three, four. She counted the seconds under her breath. And then Izzy appeared. Ten seconds. That was fast... reckless even, Kate thought as she watched them clear the zigzag rails and thunder over the low gate, pounding up the hill to the stone wall.

Nick looked serious as Izzy drew to a halt beside him. "I don't know what you two are playing at," he said at last. "You rode like maniacs out there. You paid no attention to my advice. You know your aim should be to ride competently. You appeared to be trying to break your necks in order to beat each other. I was going to suggest we practise the log pile, but I think we should now get back to the yard." His voice was icy with disgust.

"But Nick," argued Kate. "You said we could ride till four."

"I think I've seen enough of your riding for one day," he replied. "You need to rethink your attitudes if you want me to continue training either of you. Meet me in the tack room tomorrow at nine. I'm not going to say any more now. I haven't got the time. Sarah and I are going out for dinner tonight."

He turned Whispering Silver to the gate, leaving the two girls looking at each other. It was a few moments before either of them spoke.

At last Izzy began, "I suppose he's right. We did ride too fast out there."

Secretly Kate agreed, but there was no way she

was going to admit it.

Izzy waited for a few moments for Kate to reply but Kate's lips were pinched tight. Shrugging her shoulders, Izzy turned to the gate.

So what? Kate thought to herself. Why should she talk to Izzy? If Izzy had never come to Sandy Lane, Kate wouldn't have had anyone to compete with, would she?

She walked Feather through the gate. She knew she'd ridden dangerously, and felt guilty, however much she tried to ignore it. She was also well aware that it was she who had set the precedent. She wondered fleetingly about saying something to clear the air... then noticed the defiant expression on Izzy's face. No. She'd leave things as they were.

"I'm sorry Feather," Kate whispered, as she jumped down in the yard and led the little Arab into her box. "I know I pushed you."

Feather snickered softly as if in response and Kate picked up the body brush to groom her coat. She worked on Feather's back for some time, both to compensate and to ease her conscience, and then went across the yard to collect Feather's haynet.

"Kate," Izzy's voice echoed tentatively.

Kate didn't answer, and the call came again, louder this time. "Kate!"

Kate spun around. What did Izzy want? No one else was in sight. The others must have gone home.

"Midnight's behaving really strangely." Kate had never heard Izzy sound like this: beseeching and anxious at the same time. "Come and have a look at him? Please?"

"Maybe," Kate answered, warily. Her curiosity got the better of her. "What's wrong?"

"He's really restless. Not happy. He'll hardly let me near him."

Kate looked into the box. Inside, the horse's head was bent towards the floor and his ears were laid right back.

Kate was puzzled. She slid back the bolt and slipped inside. Gently, she held out her hand to try to soothe him but Midnight bared his teeth.

"He's not in a good mood tonight, are you old boy?" she said, patting his shoulder. "He's probably just tired – you did push him quite hard out there."

"Well if you hadn't forced me–" And then Izzy stopped herself and looked embarrassed.

Izzy's outburst took Kate by surprise. Were Izzy's nerves as raw as her own?

When Izzy spoke again, she sounded calmer. "I was going to speak to Nick before he goes out," she said. "But if it's nothing, I'd feel so stupid... perhaps I'll leave it."

Kate shrugged, turning away. So Izzy had taken that decision out of her hands. Good. She, like Izzy, could do without seeing Nick again that night.

Chapter 9

Panic-stricken

Kate couldn't stop thinking about Midnight. She'd dismissed Izzy's fears without thinking about him. What if there *was* something wrong? What if she'd let her irritation with Izzy get in the way? Nick had always said that if anything was wrong with one of the horses, they were to tell him straight away.

"Kate?" she heard her mother call as she walked in. "Where have you been? You said you'd be back by four thirty. You know I worry about you cycling home in the dark."

Kate sighed. "Sorry Mum," she said, putting her head around the kitchen door. "There was something wrong with one of the horses at the yard. And – well, anyway, I'm sorry."

"Just don't be late again," her mother said. "Or let me know where you are at least."

"OK." She knew her Mum was right, and besides, Kate was happy to agree to anything to escape a lecture.

"Come and have your supper. Dad and I are off out in a moment. I must get ready. Where's Alex? Alex, your food's getting cold."

Kate washed her hands in the kitchen sink, scrubbing away at the dirt under her nails.

"Where are you going, Mum?"

"The Bicknells'," her mother said over her shoulder, running upstairs. "We won't be back late."

"OK," Kate called, as Alex sat down at the table.

"Alex," she started. "I'm a bit worried about Midnight. He was very unsettled when I left. Izzy really pushed him over the cross-country. He was very tired, and then he wouldn't eat anything and..."

"Not that horse again," Alex groaned. "Leave it alone, Kate. It's none of your business. It's not as though Izzy is your friend.

"It's not Izzy I'm worried about," Kate snapped. "It's the horse. I don't care about her."

"That's abundantly clear."

"What do you mean, Alex?" Kate said, laying down her knife and fork.

"Well, you haven't been all that nice to her, have you?"

"Huh! She's not exactly the nicest person we've ever met, is she?"

"She's not bad," Alex said.

"*She's not bad?* She's dreadful. She's so conceited. All she cares about is winning at Mapletree."

"Sounds like someone else I know," Alex said.

Kate got up from the table and walked off, tears pricking her eyes. How could he? How could her own brother take the side of a complete stranger?

"I didn't expect you to understand, Alex."

"What's going on?" Mrs. Hardy asked, walking through the kitchen.

"Nothing," Kate answered.

"Do I believe you?" Mrs. Hardy said, but with a good humoured smile. "We're off in a moment. Alex, you're in charge."

"Fine," Alex said, a fake-evil grin spreading across his face. "Did you hear that Kate?"

Kate grimaced at him as he collapsed in the sitting room to watch TV.

"Call me on my mobile if you need me," their mother said, as she always did. "Bye."

Kate was still thinking about Midnight. What if something *was* wrong with him? If only she could check. Perhaps she should go back to the yard...

"Alex." Kate raced in to the sitting room.

"Sssh." He motioned to his lips, his eyes glued to the TV.

"I have to talk to you." She planted herself between Alex and the screen.

"You're in the way."

Kate thought hard. There was no point in expecting him to listen when he was in this sort of mood. "I'm going back to the stables to check on Midnight," she said. "I won't be long." She could probably slip out, and he'd hardly notice.

But Alex was immediately alert. "You're crazy, Kate. Mum would be furious. It's pitch black out there. Night time."

"She need never know," Kate said defiantly.

Before Alex could stop her, Kate was out of the house and on her bike.

"Kate." She could hear Alex crying out as she cycled away, the beam from her lights marking a faint path through the night. It was inky black, but she refused to let herself be frightened.

As she shot up the drive to the stables, she listened hard. All was quiet. She'd been silly, panicking unnecessarily. Of course there wasn't anything wrong. Relief spread over her.

Then she heard a loud moaning sound. She could tell instantly it was the sound of an animal in pain, and it was coming from Midnight's stable. A high-pitched whinny filled the air. She dropped off her bike and belted across the yard to his box.

Midnight stood bathed in sweat. The whites of his eyes were rolling viciously and the veins on his neck were jutting out like twisted cords. Desperately he lashed out, his hind legs striking the timbered walls behind him with a dull thud. Kate's heart sank. He was ill, desperately ill. Manically he plunged to the ground in sinking motions, his legs buckling beneath him. Up and down... up and down, he reeled.

What could she do? She tried Nick and then Sarah's phones with increasing worry. Both were switched off. Who else could she call? She was terrified of what might happen, but she had to think straight. "Keep calm," she told herself. "Call the vet."

Quickly, she let herself into the tack room and flicked on the light. The vet's number was on the notice board. She picked up the landline and punched out the digits.

"Hurry! Hurry!" she cried impatiently, shifting her weight from one foot to the other as it rang endlessly. At last, as she was giving up hope, preparing to leave a message, it was answered.

"This is an emergency," she said rapidly.

"OK. What's this about? I'm out on a call, right now."

Kate's heart sank. He couldn't come immediately, then. "One of the horses at Sandy Lane is ill. I don't know what to do." Panic rose in her throat. "He's going crazy. He looks as though he'll kick the box down any second."

"Slow down. Tell me what the horse is doing. Take a deep breath."

Kate didn't know where to start. "He's kicking at the walls and he keeps rolling around on the ground," she said, uncertainly. "And he's making this scary groaning noise."

"How long has this been going on?"

"I don't know," Kate cried. "I've only just got here, but his coat is drenched in sweat."

"Have you taken his temperature?"

"I can't. I don't know how to do it," Kate wailed, feeling useless.

"It sounds like colic. I'll come as soon as I can. I should be with you in half an hour."

Kate looked at her phone. That wasn't until quarter past eight. She'd have to manage until then.

"You have to keep calm," the vet stated. "Can you put a head collar on the horse and keep him from rolling? He could get stuck on his back otherwise, and it'll be hard to get him up."

"I'll try. Will he be OK?"

"I hope so," the vet said, gently. "Put a blanket on him to keep him warm. He's in a lot of pain at the moment. Imagine if you had very bad stomach ache – that's what it feels like. The pain comes in waves."

As Kate put the phone down, she felt strangely detached. She couldn't hear any more sounds – maybe the pain had eased. Quietly she approached the box and looked in. Midnight didn't even look up as she stood there.

'The pain comes in waves,' the vet had said.

Softly she drew back the bolt on his stable so as not to startle him. She held out her hand as she approached his shoulder, hiding the head collar behind her back.

"Easy does it, boy," she crooned, edging forward. She put a blanket over him successfully, but every time she tentatively reached up with the head collar, he lurched away.

The minutes passed. He was getting restless, trying to bite at his flanks. Kate knew in her heart of hearts that there was only one person who could help. She took one last look at the horse before heading for the tack room. Searched for Izzy's home phone number. There it was.

For the second time that night she punched out a number with an urgency she'd never had before, willing someone to answer the phone.

"Hi."

It was Izzy. Kate was flooded with relief.

"Izzy, it's Kate."

"Yes?" Izzy said, in an uncertain voice.

Kate's initial reaction was to clam up. Then she let the story spill out. There was deathly silence. Maybe Izzy hadn't understood... until Kate heard a muffled whimper.

"I'll be right there," Izzy whispered and the line went dead.

When Kate got back to the box, Midnight was lying down. As she drew back the bolt, he struggled to his feet, wobbling from side to side. She had to get that head collar on him.

"I know you're in pain, but the vet will be here soon," murmured Kate. She stroked his nose; maybe she could do the head collar now. "Easy does it," she began, then cried, "NO!"

His legs were beginning to buckle beneath him.

Midnight was on the floor, rolling in acute agony. That was how Izzy found him when she raced into the yard. Kate felt a pang of sympathy at the sight of Izzy's tear-stained face.

"Midnight, my Midnight," Izzy cried. The horse

struggled to his feet. "When will the vet be here? What did he say we should do?"

"We've got to get the head collar on him and he mustn't roll."

"OK," said Izzy. "Let's do it."

Slowly, Izzy reached up to the horse's neck and, with a competent hand, slid the head collar on over his head. "That's the easy part," she said grimly, turning to Kate. "There's no way we'll be able to keep him standing."

"Yes, we will," Kate said, sounding more confident than she felt. "You stand on his left, and I'll stand on his right. OK?"

"Will he die?" Izzy asked quickly.

"I don't know," Kate answered truthfully.

"It's my fault," Izzy muttered under her breath. "I'll never forgive myself."

"You mustn't think like that," Kate comforted.

Izzy was almost beyond comfort. "Where is the vet?" she cried. "It's half eight. I thought you said he'd be here at a quarter past."

"I was estimating," Kate said, through gritted teeth, trying to keep calm.

"I'm sorry," Izzy apologised. They exchanged a quick mutual glance of sympathy.

At last the vet's car rattled into the yard.

"Where are Nick and Sarah?" he asked, taking the horse's temperature.

"They're out," Kate answered.

"Unfortunate this should happen the one evening they're not around," he grimaced.

The two girls waited silently for the vet's verdict. He looked thoughtful as he tapped the thermometer and got out his stethoscope. Midnight's eyes were flecked white as the vet listened to his chest and then his abdomen.

"You did well to call me," he said.

"How did it happen?" Izzy cried.

"Sometimes it's from exercising heavily on a full stomach. Has he come in from a heavy ride today?"

The two girls looked at each other.

"What did he have to eat?" The vet hadn't noticed

their stricken faces. "Did he have a big feed?"

"The normal amount," Kate answered.

"It wasn't the normal amount," Izzy faltered. "I've been increasing his feeds."

"You have?" Kate couldn't believe it.

"I thought giving him more food would build up his energy levels. And I did ride him really hard." Her face was taut with concern.

"Did Nick tell you to do this?" asked the vet.

"No." whispered Izzy, ashamed. She could hardly get her words out. "I just thought..."

"It wasn't sensible, obviously, but try not to worry." Quickly, he extracted a syringe from his bag. "This is a painkiller and muscle relaxant," he explained, injecting the horse's neck. "The effects should be quick, but you have to watch him for the next couple of hours. He should calm down and be more at ease. Will you both be OK? I have another emergency to get to."

Kate and Izzy looked at each other.

"Keep him in his stable. Don't give him any food

tonight, but make sure he has water and ring immediately if he starts to look distressed again."

"You don't need to stay, Kate," Izzy said, when the vet had gone. "I can manage on my own."

"I'd like to, if you don't mind," Kate offered hesitantly. "It's partly my fault. If I hadn't been so desperate to race you over the cross-country, you might not have pushed him so hard."

"Oh Kate," said Izzy. "We've been so silly."

The two girls half smiled at each other, embarrassed by their admissions.

"Please stay," said Izzy. "I'd like that. I know we haven't been the best of friends, but we could try, couldn't we?"

Kate nodded, feeling awkward. She'd never been good at talking about her feelings, and didn't know what to say.

"I'd better phone Alex and tell him what's happened," she said, changing the subject. She drew out her mobile. Alex wasn't going to be in a good mood. His phone rang... once, twice, and then a pinched voice answered at the other end.

"Kate. Where are you? I've been worried sick."

"I'm OK. I'm at the stables. Midnight's really ill. He's got colic."

"Colic!"

"Yes colic," Kate answered. "I called the vet. Izzy's here too, but I've got to stay with her. Are Mum and Dad back?"

"Not yet, but what am I going to say to them when they do get back?"

"Don't worry, I'll be home before then," Kate said, feeling exhausted.

"Well, if you're not, I'll just have to think of something," Alex said, kindly.

"Thanks," Kate said gratefully. That was so like Alex. He might be annoying, but underneath all that, she knew she could count on his support. Kate turned back to concentrate on Midnight. Izzy was standing still, patiently comforting him. He looked terrible. His head hung low and his coat was clumped in whorls, but at least he was calmer.

"The vet was right, it does seem to be easing off," Izzy said.

"He looks shattered," Kate answered, patting his shoulder. "Don't you boy?"

Izzy took a deep breath. "Thank you for all you've done, Kate," she said.

"That's OK. There's something I need to say, Izzy. I'm sorry I was so unfriendly when you first came to Sandy Lane. It's just that I felt you were unfriendly too, and I couldn't bear the idea of someone else entering for Mapletree. We didn't give ourselves a chance, did we?"

"You're right," said Izzy. The two girls gave each other a steady glance.

"Quits?" Kate asked.

Izzy nodded.

They sat down in the straw, watching the black horse. And that was how Nick found them when he returned to the stables at almost midnight. They had a lot of explaining to do...

Chapter 10

A Change of Heart

"So he's eating properly now, is he?" Kate looked across her bedroom to where Izzy lay sprawled over the floor.

"Just about," Izzy answered, flicking through the pages of a pony magazine. "I thought he was going to die," she went on. "I'd never have forgiven myself if he had."

It was three days since the unforgettable evening Kate had discovered Midnight with colic. He had made a full recovery. Slowly, the two girls were getting to know each other.

Kate had been in deep trouble when her parents had returned to find her not there. Alex had tried to make excuses for her, but they'd driven straight out to the stables and brought her home. The result had been instant grounding. She'd been expecting it, but she hated being banned from Sandy Lane. Izzy gave her a daily progress report which was better than nothing, but it wasn't the same as charting his recovery with her own eyes.

"He finished off all of his haynet this evening, Kate," Izzy started. "How are you doing, stuck at home?"

"I'm bored but OK," Kate answered glumly. "I'll be glad to be going back to school tomorrow. First time in my life I've ever said that! I can't believe you didn't get into trouble for being out so late. Your parents must be so much cooler than mine."

Izzy turned a bright shade of red. Kate stared at her. Under this gaze, Izzy felt she had to say something. Finally she muttered, "I never told them I'd been out."

"What?" Kate couldn't believe it.

Izzy took a deep breath. "They never realized I'd left the house. I climbed out of my bedroom window you see," she said, nonchalantly. "They didn't even notice I was gone."

"Are you serious?"

Now Izzy had started, she found she desperately wanted to tell Kate everything, but she wasn't sure how Kate would react. A nagging voice in her head told her Kate would be horrified by the tale of deception about Midnight. A confession would spoil things. She was sure of it. Yet she *had* to tell.

Izzy paced the room. She took a deep breath. "Kate," she began. "I... um... There's something you must know," she said in a rush.

Kate giggled. "What dark secrets are you hiding? Murder? Robbery? Come on then, tell me all."

"I don't know where to start really," Izzy said, in a shaky voice.

Kate looked startled. "It can't be that bad, can it?"

"It is—"

Izzy started speaking uncontrollably fast. Once she'd started, she couldn't stop, and in less than a minute she'd blurted out the whole story – how she'd seen the advert about Midnight, how she'd grown to love him, how she had had to turn down Mrs. Charlwood's offer to have him as a gift, and then the plan she'd made to keep Midnight.

"So you see, I just have to win at the trials," Izzy went on. "Everything's riding on it. If I don't, I won't be able to pay Nick what I owe him."

Kate was silent for a moment as she took it all in.

"Say something, Kate," Izzy begged.

"I just don't know what to say," Kate stammered. "I can't believe it. I just can't believe you had the nerve to do it. And you haven't told your parents any of this?"

"Are you crazy? Of course I haven't," said Izzy. "Although they know that I'm riding in a horse trials on Saturday."

"Who do they think you're riding?" Kate enquired.

"I told them that Mrs. Charlwood had decided to

send Midnight to the stables I've been going to, and that I've been picked to ride him," Izzy started.

"And they believed you?" Kate looked astonished.

"It's sort of true, Kate," Izzy pleaded. "The only thing I haven't told them is that I'm supposed to be paying his livery fees."

"So that makes it all right then, does it?" Kate asked. She was deeply shocked. Izzy had deliberately deceived her parents! But she also understood how Izzy's feelings for Midnight had carried her away. As she stared at her friend's pale face, she felt sorry for her. Izzy looked sick with worry, and now Kate noticed great dark shadows ringed her eyes.

"But even if you do win at Mapletree," Kate found herself saying, having reached a dire but obvious conclusion, "It's not going to be enough to pay for a livery fee forever, is it?"

"I know... I know that now," Izzy cried. "I didn't think about it at the time. I was so desperate, I didn't think it through. I guessed I'd be able to work out a way to earn the rest of the money later, somehow.

What would *you* have done?" Izzy asked. "Would you have just sat by and let Midnight be sold?"

"Probably not." Kate looked thoughtful. "Anyway, it's not helpful to go down that road. We've got to sort this out."

What would she have done though? Kate wondered. Deep down, she knew she wouldn't have had the guts to do what Izzy had done. For the first time, she felt a stirring of admiration for the girl who sat in front of her, pouring her heart out.

"Let's get this straight," Kate tried to make sense of the facts. "Your parents know that you've been coming to Sandy Lane, they just don't know that Midnight's your horse."

"Yes," said Izzy, waiting for Kate to come up with a solution.

Kate took a deep breath. "I think you should tell your parents before Mapletree–"

"*Tell my parents*?" Izzy cried. "But I can't, they'll go mad."

"They're going to find out sooner or later, aren't

they? Wouldn't it be better if you told them now, before it gets any worse? They'll know what to do," said Kate.

"They're bound to make me sell Midnight," Izzy said, mournfully.

"But if you don't tell your parents, and you don't win at Mapletree, you won't even have the money to pay Nick and Sarah for his livery fee. At least if you tell your parents, they might help you out before you dig yourself in any deeper."

"I know. I know you're right." Izzy hung her head. "But you don't know my parents. It's not going to be that easy."

"Look," Kate said in a reassuring voice. "If you explain it all to them, the way you've explained it to me, they'll have to understand. Yes, they're going to be furious at first, but if you tell them that the prize money from Mapletree will cover you for a month's livery and that you're sure to win, they might soften and pay for the rest of his stabling," Kate said, sounding more confident than she felt.

"Not a chance," Izzy said glumly. "You don't know my parents, Kate–"

"Kate, Kate." Alex's voice boomed up the stairs, drawing their conversation to a close. "Supper!"

"Sorry about that," Kate said quickly. "You'd better go. We'll talk about this another time. Think about what I've said. You'll feel much better once you've told them. You've got nothing to lose, have you?"

"I suppose you're right," Izzy said. Kate's words were comforting. It had been a relief to confess. Maybe her parents would understand too. She was filled with new resolve.

"I'll do it. But please don't tell any of the others about all this?" Izzy whispered as they headed for the door. "I couldn't bear it if they knew."

"Don't worry," Kate promised.

As Izzy stepped outside, Kate's words rang in her ears. *'You've got nothing to lose.'* Izzy stopped in her tracks. But she had, hadn't she? They might make her sell Midnight. She had everything to lose.

Chapter 11

An Unexpected Reaction

A whole school week had gone by since Izzy had spoken with Kate, and still she hadn't done anything about telling her parents. She kept getting texts from Kate, asking her if she'd done it. But there hadn't been a suitable moment.

Kate's texts were beginning to sound impatient. "*Get on with it.*" And "*The right time is NOW!*"

"*OK. Promise.*" That was the last text she'd sent back. Since then, the girls hadn't spoken.

Now it was early Saturday morning: the day of the Mapletree show. She didn't have much time if she was going to keep her promise.

Izzy sighed as she walked through the house. Her mother was having a bath, but judging from sounds of tapping on computer keys coming from the study, her father was busy writing. Twice Izzy walked up to the study to rap on the door, only to walk away again. She felt as though she was standing at the edge of a precipice waiting to jump. OK, she told herself. Now or never. Boldly, she turned the handle. Inside, she saw her father typing rapidly.

"What is it Izzy? I'm quite busy," he said.

"Um, could I have a word, please Dad?" she said, nervously.

"Is this important?" he asked, not glancing up from his computer.

"Yes," Izzy answered. "Yes it is." She clenched her fists and took a deep breath.

Her father held up his hand before she started. "I know what I meant to tell you," he said. "I got a call yesterday from a chap at that stables you've been going to – someone called Nick?"

Izzy's heart began to beat double time. So Nick had found out already. Had Kate told him? She opened her mouth to say something and closed it again. She couldn't think of an excuse.

"I'm sorry Dad. I'm really sorry. I—"

"Sorry?" Mr. Paterson looked up, bemused. "Whatever for? I rather liked him actually. He wanted to know if your mother and I wanted tickets to watch you ride at this horse show thing this morning. He seemed quite impressed by you... said you were pretty good, Izzy."

Mr. Paterson smiled at his daughter. "This is the first time I've heard anyone rave about your abilities since you were at nursery school!" he said, with a laugh. "Aren't you pleased?"

Izzy couldn't bring herself to say anything as her father went on. "Anyway, I spoke to your mother and we've decided we're going to come and watch and see how you do. Perhaps there's more to this riding lark than we thought. Izzy? Are you listening?"

But Izzy was miles away. She felt as though she

was hearing everything from a distance. She had to say something before it was too late.

"Dad," she began. "Oh, it's all such a mess. I don't know where to start–"

"What is it now, Izzy?" Mr. Paterson smiled. "Must you always be so dramatic?"

"I'm not this time, Dad. Dad, you're not listening to me," Izzy cried. "You're not listening at all. I've lied. I lied to both you and Mum. Mrs. Charlwood didn't send Midnight to Sandy Lane at all – I did." Izzy blurted the words out.

"You did?" Mr. Paterson looked surprised. "What are you talking about Izzy?"

"I didn't let him go to the sale. I couldn't. I thought that if I could win at Mapletree, I could pay for his livery fees for a month, and then... and then..."

"Whoah, slow down, Izzy," Mr. Paterson's voice was dangerously careful. "Mrs. Charlwood let you do all this?"

"N-Not exactly," Izzy gulped, looking at her father who was tense with fury. "You see, I told her you'd agreed to it–"

"WHAT!" Mr. Paterson bellowed. For a moment he was lost for words, and then he started again, as the full force of Izzy's words hit home. "Does Nick know about this?" he asked. "He put you up to it?"

"No," Izzy said, quickly. "He doesn't know anything thing about it."

"You've lied to us! Very well, then, you're not riding," Mr. Paterson shouted.

"But Dad." The colour drained from Izzy's face. "I've got to. Nick's depending on it."

"He'll have to make other arrangements. He's going to think I'm a right idiot after our conversation yesterday, isn't he?" He paused for a moment. "On second thoughts, maybe you'd better ride today." Izzy looked astonished, waiting for her dad to continue with the conditions that were bound to follow. "But then that horse is going."

"But–" Izzy started. It was worse than she'd imagined possible.

"No buts," Mr. Paterson said, sternly. "I'm very

disappointed in you, Izzy, and your mother will be too. I can't believe you've lied like this."

"Please don't tell Mum yet." Tears poured down Izzy's cheeks. "Please wait until Mapletree is over."

Mr. Paterson made a snap decision. "OK. I'll do that. But she'll have to know afterwards."

Izzy hung her head, shamefully.

"You've let us down badly," Mr. Paterson said, shaking his head. "And you can phone this Nick and tell him we'll be driving you to the trials too. You're not going with the rest of the team. Now that I know what you're capable of, I wouldn't put anything past you," her father continued angrily, not allowing Izzy to interrupt.

It was all too much – the confession, the confusion, the telling-off. Before Izzy knew it, the tears were coursing down her cheeks.

"I have to phone Kate," she said, anything to escape from the room. "At least she won't be annoyed with me." She raced to her bedroom, so she could be alone and private.

Quickly, she tapped in Kate's number. And then her heart sank as it quickly went to voicemail. Kate was chatting to someone else.

She pressed 'end call' in despair. She didn't leave a message. All she wanted to do was curl up in bed. She wiped her eyes with her sleeve. It didn't matter if she won or lost at Mapletree now – she couldn't keep Midnight anyway. And yet somehow it did. Somehow it mattered very much how she rode. She had to show her parents what had made her do it. She had to prove that Midnight had been worth it.

"Come on, Kate. You ought to be nearly ready now."

"Coming Mum," she called.

Kate was slowly changing for Mapletree, but she kept getting lost in her thoughts. If she was totally honest with herself, the current silence between her and Izzy hadn't all been Izzy's fault. There was something else that had caused the tension between them – something she hadn't been able to tell Izzy.

Winning at Mapletree had filled Kate's mind for

the last few months. She'd dreamed about it, dwelt upon it, lived it, breathed it. She wanted to win more than anything in the world. And now she knew she couldn't. She had to let Izzy win. She had to let Izzy have the chance to keep her horse. She knew how much it meant to her, and there'd be plenty of other horse trials.

She wondered if Izzy had told her parents yet.

Would they be as understanding as she'd said they would be? What if they weren't? Kate knew that it was only at her urging that Izzy was telling them.

Kate's head was spinning now, and there was a gnawing, sick feeling in the pit of her stomach. What would Nick say when she messed things up? Hadn't he said before that if Feather won, it would make her a more valuable horse? Still, Kate's mind was made up. She and Feather were not going to win. To help Izzy, they just couldn't.

Chapter 12

Mapletree

Kate came downstairs wearing her new navy show jacket and went into the kitchen where her mother was pouring a cup of tea.

"All right, Kate?" she asked. "Feeling nervous?"

"Not too bad," Kate answered, with a shrug.

"You look smart, Kate," Alex said, bounding in. "All set and raring to go? Not nervous?"

"I'm fine," she snapped.

"Grumpy! Last minute nerves," he whispered to his mother, but Kate heard him. She wished everyone would stop talking about nerves.

"What time are you leaving for the stables?" her mother went on.

"Whenever Alex is ready," replied Kate. "I'm ready to go now."

It was a clear, crisp day. Perfect weather for riding. Under normal circumstances, Kate would have been delighted to be going to a horse trials, but today was not going to be normal.

She checked her appearance in the mirror. That would have to do. Fleetingly she wondered again about Izzy and her parents. She'd had a missed call from her, but she hadn't rung her back. Deliberately riding badly at Mapletree was enough for her to cope with.

"Come on, Kate," Alex called. "We don't want to be late."

Grabbing her riding hat, she followed Alex out of the house.

"Nervous Izzy?" her mother asked.

"A bit," she answered. She felt a fraud pretending

to her mother that everything was all right when it wasn't.

"Can we go soon?" she asked, hoping to change the conversation.

"Why? What's the hurry? Your dressage test isn't till eleven is it?" her mother answered.

"No, but I want to watch Kate in hers," Izzy answered. "She's on at nine, so the sooner I'm there the better."

"OK, OK. I'll call your dad, and we'll start. Max! Max! We're ready!"

"One minute." A reply came from the depths of his study.

"Come on, Max. This is Izzy's day," Mrs. Paterson said, smiling. Izzy reddened as her father's glance fell on her; a stern look hard as iron.

Izzy twisted uncomfortably in her hacking jacket. It was Kate's old one, and just too tight for her. She wished she was wearing her scruffy, familiar old fleece.

At last they were ready and in the car, seatbelts

snapped in. Mr. Paterson started the car and pulled out of the drive.

"Shall we set the satnav?" Mrs. Paterson asked. "Do you know where we're going, Izzy?"

"I've looked it up," Izzy answered, opening the road atlas beside her. "We need to take the road to Ash Hill, carry on through Belmont, and then it's straight all the way to Mapletree." She tucked a strand of hair behind her ear as she spoke.

"Easy then," her mother said. "We should be there in plenty of time. So why don't you tell us how these trials work then, Izzy."

An uncomfortable silence pervaded the car. Izzy decided to ignore it. She took a deep breath and attempted to make a start. "OK," she began. "The main event of the day is the Open Cup. There'll be a load of older riders competing for that. It's the last qualifying event for the Trentdown Trials. I'm in the Junior Cup for under 12s. It's a new sort of event – the first of its kind to be held at Mapletree. You ride in dressage, showjumping and cross-country and the scores in each of them are then added up."

All this talk had taken up her attention. Izzy never noticed the traffic stacking up ahead of them. She looked at her phone and frowned. It was already a quarter to nine.

"Uh oh," her mother sighed.

"What is it?" Izzy asked, looking up and seeing for herself the massive queue ahead.

"I knew we should have left earlier," she cried, as they drew up behind a large trailer and came to a grinding halt. "I'm going to miss Kate's dressage."

"Be patient, Izzy," her mother said, calmly. "I'm sure it'll get going in a minute."

But Mrs. Paterson's words didn't reassure her.

"It's not far now. Look there you are," Mrs. Paterson pointed. "Horse Trials one mile."

"But the traffic's not moving. I'm going to have to get out and walk," Izzy wailed.

"You'll do no such thing." Mr. Paterson looked stern. "Calm down."

But Izzy was finding it hard to sit still. She should

have known something like this would happen. Vacantly, she stared out of the window. The traffic was starting to move again and Izzy could vaguely hear the muffled sound of a loud speaker in the distance. She looked across the grass at the showjumping ring, surrounded by green and white striped stands. They hadn't even reached the entrance yet. Izzy screwed her hands up into little balls, clenching them and unclenching them.

"Sorry," she gasped. "It's five to nine. I have to get out. I'll see you by the secretary's tent at half eleven."

And before they could stop her, Izzy had undone her seat belt, leapt out of the car, and was running blindly down the road. Sprinting along the grass verge, she pushed past people hurrying to the trials on foot.

"Excuse me, excuse me," she cried, stumbling forward as she raced. She knew she should stop and ask someone where she'd find the dressage arena, but she couldn't waste time slowing down for that.

And then it all happened so quickly. One minute

she was hurtling forward, the next she had put her foot in a hole, and was crashing to the ground.

"Ow!" She grimaced, rubbing her ankle.

"Are you OK?" a woman called over.

"I'm fine," Izzy said, angry with herself for falling. She didn't want to waste more time.

She forced herself to get to her feet and gasped. A sharp, searing pain shot through her foot. Tears sprang up in her eyes as she struggled to stand.

"I'll be all right in a moment," she said to the woman, wincing as she tried to put some weight on the injured foot.

"I don't think you will be. It looks as though you've twisted your ankle."

Wheezing to catch her breath, Izzy looked at her phone. It was two minutes past nine. Too late. She'd have missed Kate's test, and now the tears she'd desperately been trying to hold back all morning, began to run down her face.

"I'm late to see my friend ride," she explained. "And I'm going to lose my horse too. I so wanted my parents to see how good he was," she babbled. "My ankle's throbbing, and I'm supposed to be in the dressage arena at eleven."

"Don't worry," the lady said kindly. "I think we'd better get you to the first aid tent as quickly as possible. Put your arm over my shoulder and lean on me. There, that's it. Somehow I don't think you'll be riding today."

As Kate came out of the ring, she hoped against hope that Nick hadn't seen her performance. She had certainly ridden badly enough to whisk Feather and herself out of any chance of a prize. Her first circle had been more of a square and then she had circled at C instead of E – that was two penalty points straight off for a change of course. Feather had swished her tail and seemed confused, but still she had obeyed Kate's instructions.

At least it was all over. She'd have to forget it. It had definitely been humiliating to put on such a poor performance. Looking up, Kate saw Alex heading straight for her.

"You were really bad. Terrible. What happened?" he demanded, in his typical blunt style.

"An attack of nerves?" Kate said quickly, turning away so that he couldn't see her face.

"You're lying eighth. You've completely blown it, Kate. I thought you'd be up there with the leaders after the dressage."

"I know, I know, don't keep going on about it, Alex," Kate said hastily, jumping to the ground and burying her head in Feather's neck. "Where's Nick?" she asked anxiously.

"Not sure." Alex looked blank. "He said he'd be watching, but no way will he congratulate you with that display."

"Any sign of Izzy?" Kate asked, blanking out his sharp comment.

"She hasn't come," Alex said. "We've all been wondering where she's got to. Nick said she'd be here by nine."

"Probably hasn't told her parents yet," Kate

muttered under her breath.

"What was that?" Alex asked.

"Nothing," Kate answered tiredly. Izzy had let her down. She had given up so much to give her friend a good chance of winning – Nick's opinion of her, Feather's future, her own opportunities. And Izzy didn't even have the basic good manners to turn up on time.

Kate was kicking a stone around the ground when she heard the announcement over the speaker that set her worrying again.

"Could the parents of Izzy Paterson come to the first aid tent immediately?"

What was going on? She had to know. Instantly, she set off, darting this way and that, dodging in and out of the crowds as she ran. Stopping for a moment to catch her breath, Kate caught sight of the first aid tent and plunged inside.

Izzy wasn't alone. Nick was already there and a nurse hovered in the background. Kate could hear drifts of Nick's words.

"So that's it. Their final decision. I'm afraid you're not going to be able to ride Midnight, Izzy..."

Izzy not riding Midnight? What was wrong with her? Kate blinked.

"Kate." Nick looked grim. "You've come at the right time. I wanted to see you. I'm sorry I missed you and Feather, but I heard the result. What have you got to say about that?"

"I didn't do well," Kate said, quietly. No point in defending herself. "Six penalty points."

"And I'm afraid Izzy's twisted her ankle," Nick explained. "That's the end of her hopes on Midnight."

"Izzy! How did that happen?" Kate cried.

"I was late getting here," Izzy said. Her face was stained with tears. "We were stuck in traffic, so I leapt out of the car and was racing as fast as I could go and... I fell. That's not the point, though. Nick's got something to say to you."

Half puzzled, half apprehensive, Kate looked at Nick, waiting for his explanation.

"It's quite simple," said Nick. "You've clearly

brought your chances with Feather to a definite close; I don't understand why, because you can ride better than that. So I suggested to Izzy that you take over from her and ride Midnight. Izzy's agreed, but it's up to you. Do you want to? I'm sorry, but I can't give you much time to make your mind up."

Kate looked from one face to the other. She didn't know what to say.

Izzy said, and her voice was very gentle. "I'd like you to ride him. I can't, and besides, it'll give you a second chance at the trophy."

A second chance at the trophy. Kate was torn between being devastated for Izzy and thrilled for herself. She knew the right answer now.

"I'll do it," she said, determinedly.

"Good. I'll leave you both to discuss Midnight," smiled Nick. "I have to get permission for the change of rider at the secretary's tent." He turned to Kate. "Meet me at the horse box in exactly half an hour."

Kate nodded. As soon as he'd gone, she turned back to Izzy. "Do you mind?" she asked.

"It's fine, Kate," Izzy assured her. "It makes no difference now."

"What do you mean?" Kate couldn't understand the sadness, the hopelessness in Izzy's tone. "Everything depends on it."

"Not now," Izzy replied. "I told Dad everything, and he was really furious with me. He's going to make me sell Midnight anyway. It wouldn't matter if I won or came last, so don't think about me. You go out there and do your best for your own sake."

"Sure I'll do that Izzy, but–"

Izzy held up her hand to silence her friend. "There's nothing more to be done," she said. She sounded tired, as though she'd staggered to the end of an uphill run. "I can't bear to talk about it any more. Now I'm going to have to wait for my parents to explain what's happened."

Kate was full of pity, but she didn't have the words to say all she felt. She touched her friend on the shoulder and left the tent.

Chapter 13

Showjumping

The showjumping ring stood quiet and empty as the last of the competitors finished their tests over at the dressage arena. Brightly painted flags fluttered in the breeze. Kate had ridden Midnight fairly well in the dressage – they were lying in third place, but there was still a long way to go. Kate wondered how Izzy was. She hadn't turned up to watch her. Maybe she was having a tough time with her parents.

Ducking under the railings, Kate looked carefully at the course. The jumps weren't enormous by showjumping standards, but she would need to jump them clear if she wanted to catch up with the leader. She was quiet as she walked the course, contemplating it all. She looked at her phone – nearly time now. She had to go and tack up Midnight. Quickly, she headed back to the horse box. The showground was busy, as she went on her way, each of the riders getting ready for their different events.

"You ought to go and limber up," Nick called over to where she stood. "You're on in the showjumping ring in twenty minutes."

"I know," Kate answered, hurrying to Midnight, tightening the girth and jumping into the saddle.

As she walked over to the collecting ring, she ran over the course in her mind. She felt strangely apart from the trials as she watched – like someone in a dream – the riders popping over the practice jump. Kate took a deep breath. Poor Izzy... She had to do well now, for Izzy's sake. She had to show everyone what Midnight could do.

They were up to number twenty-two – just two

more riders ahead of her. Time was going painfully slowly. She couldn't bear it; she wished it was over and done with. Now she trotted quietly over to the ring, awaiting her turn. Then she heard Midnight's number being announced and rode into the arena. As the sound of the bell echoed around the grounds, she pushed Midnight onto the first.

"Come on, my boy," she cried, urging him onto the brush. The black horse responded willingly and they cleared the jump with ease. Kate rode him hard at the shark's teeth. Touchdown and clear, and now it was the combination.

Carefully, she eased him over the fence. Clear! Now onto the parallel bars. They glided over the jump in quick, easy strides and headed for the triple. Jump... clear, jump... clear, jump... clear.

The crowd was quiet as the pair soared over the jumps in swift succession. Midnight didn't even hesitate as Kate rode him around the course. He snorted excitedly in the run-up to the gate and landed lightly. There were only two jumps left between them and a clear round.

Kate turned Midnight for the stile, and he soared over the jump with inches to spare. Now there was only the wall. Kate didn't hesitate as she swung Midnight wide, giving him enough berth to look at the jump. Midnight coursed through the air as if it were invisible, and they cantered through the finish to a round of applause.

Almost immediately Kate was surrounded by a circle of excited faces.

"Clear round, Kate," the Sandy Lane team cried.

"Yes, well done, Kate," said Nick. Kate smiled weakly. Anxiously, she looked around her as she jumped to the ground.

"Have you seen Izzy?" she asked Alex.

"She's with her parents," he answered, raising his eyebrows. "It seems they have a lot to discuss."

"Do you know what?" Kate asked, nervously.

"Not exactly" said Alex. "She muttered something about Midnight's livery fees."

"Nothing else?"

"What else could there be?" Alex said. Suspicion dawned on him "Are you and Izzy up to something?"

Kate avoided his eye, and didn't reply. She was concentrating on leading Midnight off by the reins. Then she was going to find Izzy.

Chapter 14

Cross-country

It didn't take Kate long to find Izzy, nor for Izzy to tell her what had happened. When her parents had arrived at the first aid tent, after their initial burst of sympathy for her ankle, they'd given her a difficult time. She'd had a lot of explaining to do, after her father had informed her mother of her deception. Mrs. Paterson had been very angry. She couldn't believe Izzy had lied so consistently. She'd been as adamant as Izzy's father that Midnight had to be sold. Unable to take the atmosphere in the tent any more, Izzy had limped away as soon as possible.

Now, as Kate and Izzy leant on the railings by the cross-country course, they both felt low. Wearily, Izzy clapped her hands together as competitor number forty-three rode through the finish to a round of applause.

"Hey. Don't be down, Kate," Izzy said. "You should be the one trying to make me feel good, not the other way round."

"I know, I know," said Kate. "I suppose I thought that your parents would want to help you, that they'd come up with something."

"They have." Izzy thought about what they'd proposed. "They've agreed to pay Nick what I owe him – nearly a month's livery fee – they've been very generous." Momentarily she felt upset. It was OK for her to criticise her parents, but she didn't like hearing someone else do it.

"They're still making you sell Midnight though," Kate observed.

Izzy shrugged her shoulders. "I knew it would happen. Why did you think there'd be any other outcome?" she asked, trying to stifle her tears and keep her voice steady. "At least you get to ride him at the trials," she added.

Izzy resents me, Kate thought. She felt hurt. "You said you wanted me to. That you didn't mind," she said. She wanted, with a sudden overwhelming urge, to tell Izzy how she had sacrificed her own chances with Feather. But she stopped herself. She didn't want Izzy hurt any more. Besides, it couldn't change things now. Then an announcement over the loud speaker interrupted her thoughts.

"And that was the leader, Justin Rolph on Light Fandango in four minutes and thirty seconds," the speaker announced.

Both friends looked up. Kate went quiet.

"Great," she said despondently. "How will I ever beat that?"

"Easily," Izzy said confidently.

"But it was so fast," said Kate.

"Yeah, but you only have to ride four minutes fifteen to make up the two points."

Kate looked doubtful. Izzy shrugged and turned away. It was a few minutes before she said anything.

"Well, you're probably right, Kate. I always felt you should have practised a lot harder at Sandy Lane – cross-country's never been your strong point, has it?" she said, looking down so that Kate couldn't see her biting her bottom lip. "I could always beat you easily," Izzy continued.

"What do you mean you could always beat me easily?" Kate was furious. Who did Izzy think she was? A riding genius? "Only because you almost broke Midnight's neck in the process," she yelled. "I'll show you how to ride really well."

She marched off, stomping across the showground, leaving Izzy standing alone. It was exactly the reaction Izzy had wanted.

"Yes, you show me how you can ride really well, Kate," she said, limping off slowly with her crutches.

Kate gritted her teeth as she and Midnight stood in the start box, patiently waiting for the official to signal the start of the cross-country. The wind was blowing up around them. She'd have to go very fast if they were to have any chance of winning. Kate held her breath. The starter counted her down, and they were off.

The cheers of the crowd echoed in her ears as they thundered over the first jump and galloped into the trees. Skirting through the woody copse, turning this way and that, Kate navigated a clear route through to the other side and then they were at the sloping rails.

"Come on, Midnight," she cried determinedly as she collected him for the log into the water. "Steady now, easy does it."

The black horse jumped into the water and splashed through the brook. Leaning forwards in the saddle, Kate urged him up the other side. His hooves sank deep into the mud as he struggled to keep his footing, but he was out clear and now they galloped the turn for the fallen tree.

She was over that. Nimbly, Kate turned for the

drop into the creek, leaning back to take the weight off Midnight's front legs, down into the dip and up the other side for the rails. The mud sprayed up in Kate's face and she spluttered, breathlessly.

It was a long, hard gallop to the next fence but she'd done OK so far; they hadn't put a foot wrong. Bracing herself for the tyres, Kate pushed her seat down deep into the saddle.

"Come on," she cried, riding hard in the approach. The gutsy black horse didn't baulk at the solid jump. With a huge leap, he hauled himself over it with inches to spare. Kate didn't even give him time to think about what he had just cleared as she turned him for the low gate and surged on over the trough. Halfway home. Kate was starting to feel confident.

Sailing over the stone wall, they headed for the next fence. Kate drove Midnight on with her heels and he rose to the challenge, tucking his legs neatly up under him. Now it was Devil's Ditch. Kate could sense that he was tiring. Down the bank, over the log pile and onto the triple bar. Kate rode at the middle of the jump, steadying Midnight for the take-off and they landed lightly.

Just two more jumps. The double oxer was now in their sights. Up and over and touchdown. They were clear. Just one more jump. The black horse swished his tail as they flew across the turf and sprinted through the finish.

Crossing the line, Kate drew to a halt and collapsed in a heap on Midnight's neck. Had she done it? Gasping to catch her breath, she didn't even look up at the sound of voices around her.

Before she knew it, she was surrounded by Nick and the Sandy Lane gang. It was some time before she'd even got her breath back to speak.

"Are you OK?" Nick asked. "Say something."

For once Kate was lost for words, struggling for air. At last she croaked, "How did I do?"

"Brilliantly. You were amazing," Alex said, as Kate slithered to the ground, her legs quivering like jelly beneath her.

"But was it enough?" she gasped.

"We have to wait and see," said Alex.

"Kate Hardy and Midnight. Four minutes and twelve seconds," the loud speaker announced.

"You've done it! You've done it!" the Sandy Lane team cried. But there was only one face Kate wanted to see.

"There," Kate said, proudly, as Izzy and her parents came up to her. "Who said I couldn't do it?"

"I didn't doubt it for a moment," Izzy grinned, patting Midnight's neck.

Suddenly light dawned. "Hey!" Kate grinned too, pointing at Izzy. "You only said it to spur me on."

"It worked didn't it?" Izzy said. "Kate, meet my mum and dad."

"Hello," Kate said, remembering her manners in front of Izzy's parents. She looked at their smiling faces. What was going on? She couldn't work it out. Izzy was smiling too – when she'd just been told she had to sell her horse. In fact she looked glowing. No trace of annoyance from her parents. And now, here were Nick and her own parents arriving to add to the crowd.

"Well done, Kate," congratulated Nick, patting Midnight's neck. "You were very good. You and Midnight excelled yourselves."

"Yes, well done, Kate," beamed her mother. Kate hugged her, then remembered there was something more pressing that she needed to know. She looked at Izzy.

"What's going on, Izzy?"

"I can keep Midnight," Izzy said, calmly.

Before Izzy had a chance to explain further, the loud speaker made another announcement.

"Kate Hardy and Midnight are the overall winners of the Junior Mapletree Cup."

"I've won? I've truly won at Mapletree?" Kate exclaimed. "I don't believe it."

"Well, you'd better believe it," said Izzy, pushing Kate into the ring. "They're waiting to present your prize. Hurry up." Izzy smiled. "Go on, they're calling your name."

"But Midnight? What happened?"

"I'll explain it all when you get back. Just get out there and collect that cup before they give it to someone else," Izzy teased. "Midnight's here to stay," she smiled. "But it's a bit of a long story..."

Kate remounted and rode off slowly, burning with curiosity. "I'll catch up with you later," she called back to Izzy as she rode into the ring. Just one single glorious fact filled her mind now. She was first at Mapletree! As she collected her cup and galloped the lap of honour, Kate could only smile.

Chapter 15

Midnight to Stay

"Yay! She won! YAY!!!!!!!"

Nick flinched at the yelling as he drove the Sandy Lane team back to the yard. But he didn't try to stop them. He was as pleased as they were– a first at Mapletree was excellent. Izzy and Kate were tucked away in the back, out of earshot of the noise in the front.

"I'm really sorry you didn't get to ride at the trials, Izzy," Kate confided.

"Never mind about all that when I can keep Midnight," Izzy answered. "There'll be loads of other trials for us."

"Tell me again how it happened – slowly this time," Kate said.

"OK." Izzy took a deep breath. "I only know what happened from Mum, but this is what she said. After I got out of the first aid tent, Dad went to find Nick. He told him all about the deception, expecting Nick to be as furious as he was, but Nick stuck up for me... said that I was a gutsy kid and had enough talent to fill a stable." Izzy blushed at the words of praise.

"And Dad couldn't believe it," Izzy went on, enthusiasm spilling out into her speech. "He was amazed that Nick believed in me so much, and then when Nick said he would be prepared to buy Midnight if Dad couldn't afford to keep him, Dad was totally swayed. He said I could have him."

"Unbelievable," said Kate.

"But there are conditions attached – it wasn't a complete breeze. Midnight and I are on a six month trial period, so I've got to work really hard at school to improve my marks, although Mum says I've as good as got him. And there was something else that helped change his mind."

Kate waited patiently as Izzy paused to analyse her father's thought process.

"I think that the details of it all intrigued him," she began. "Me wanting Midnight so badly... keeping him secret... the colic... He said it all had the makings of a great book!"

Kate laughed, and the Land Rover turned sharply into the yard.

The horses were unboxed and Midnight was back in his stable. The two girls stood leaning on the door, watching the black horse eat from his haynet.

"It is strange how things turn out, isn't it?" Izzy murmured.

"How d' you mean?" asked Kate.

"It's like this. If I hadn't seen that advert, I'd never have met Mrs. Charlwood. Never have seen Midnight. I wouldn't have found Sandy Lane, or met you... It's all chance – one thing leading to the other.

And I never thought I'd be able to keep Midnight. I know I was lucky. I shouldn't really have got away with it. And..." She paused.

"Go on. What were you about to say, Izzy?"

"It's weird how you can be so wrong about people too. Do you remember that first morning when I arrived at Sandy Lane?"

"How could I forget?" Kate answered.

"Well, you have to remember I was upset. I'd been parted from Midnight for so long," Izzy went on. "And I'd been ill, and then you were so horrible..."

"Me, horrible?"

The two girls glared at each other. It was just at that moment that Midnight lifted his head and whinnied loudly, bringing their clash to a close.

Kate looked at Izzy. Izzy looked at Kate, and they both burst out laughing.